This Book Belongs To......

....

....

Made in the USA
Monee, IL
18 November 2022

18017910R00057